D1237522

"*Sam the Eco Robot & the Ghost Nets* is a fantastic visual for young children to learn that there are simple ways to make our environment better for the future. Ms. Wanick is showing that children can do the same, such as cleaning the beaches, in a fun and exciting way."

**—Gitanjali Rao, Young Innovator,** *TIME* **"Kid of the Year" 2020**

"A wonderful and educational book for children of all ages, from two to ninety-nine! I got a copy for my grandson and I. We need to educate our children from early ages to understand the human interaction with the environment."

**—Professor Dr. Hashem Akbari, Energy, Environment, and Climate Scientist; Recipient of the 2007 Nobel Peace Prize on Climate Change shared with Former U.S. Vice President, Al Gore**

"Ms. Wanick has written a delightful children's book about caring for our planet and one another. She has long cared about environmental issues and this story encourages our young people to do the same, to be leaders in caring for Mother Earth. Inventive. Fun. Engaging, too. Bravo!"

**—Cameron Kim Dawson, Sky Dog Productions; Producer of** *Teenage Mutant Ninja Turtles I, II,* **and** *III,* **and** *The All New Mickey Mouse Club*

"The mechanical cleverness of the robot and the sounds of the recycle machines are wonderful! Children will be fascinated by all of this mechanical detail in the pictures and they will ask a lot of questions about them."

**— Dr. Pippa Goodhart, award-winning author of over one hundred children's books including the celebrated "You Choose" picture book series and This or That, created for The British Museum. Tutor at ICE, The University of Cambridge, England.**

# SAM THE ECO ROBOT

## & THE GHOST NETS

This book belongs to

_____.

WRITTEN BY: THASSANEE WANICK

ILLUSTRATED BY: TERESA & STEVEN GEER

Post Hill PRESS

A POST HILL PRESS BOOK

ISBN: 978-1-63758-305-0

Cover and interior illustrations by Teresa and Steven Geer
Typesetting and interior design by Yoni Limor

Post Hill Press
New York • Nashville
posthillpress.com

Published in the United States of America
1 2 3 4 5 6 7 8 9 10
Printed in Canada

# DEDICATION

To God for His everlasting love and this book, yet another of His miracles!

To my husband, Eduardo W. Wanick, brilliant physicist and responsible world business leader who chose to become an oceanographer after his retirement. My untiring supporter and superhero.

To my fantastic daughter with a heart of gold, Leslie Wanick French.
A Rolls Royce Aerospace Engineering Manager who also makes the world's best hazelnut chocolate cake!

To the children, our "Future Leaders" who will one day become business leaders, educators, policy makers, Presidents, and Prime Ministers.

# SAM THE ECO ROBOT

## & THE GHOST NETS

**VRRROOOMMM...VRRROOOMMM...**
Sam the Eco Robot revved up the engine of his Eco Boat while he waited for his two best friends, Jack and Jen, to go clean up plastics in the ocean.

"Hop in and let's go!" shouted Sam happily.

"Whoa! There's so much plastic trash in the ocean today," said Sam.

"Look! What's that?" Jen pointed to something wobbling far away.

"Oh, no! Those are ghost nets," said Sam.

"Ghost nets? What are they?" asked Jack.

"They are old, broken fishing nets and fish traps that fishermen threw away. They flop and float in the ocean like ghosts and trap sea creatures along the way," explained Sam.

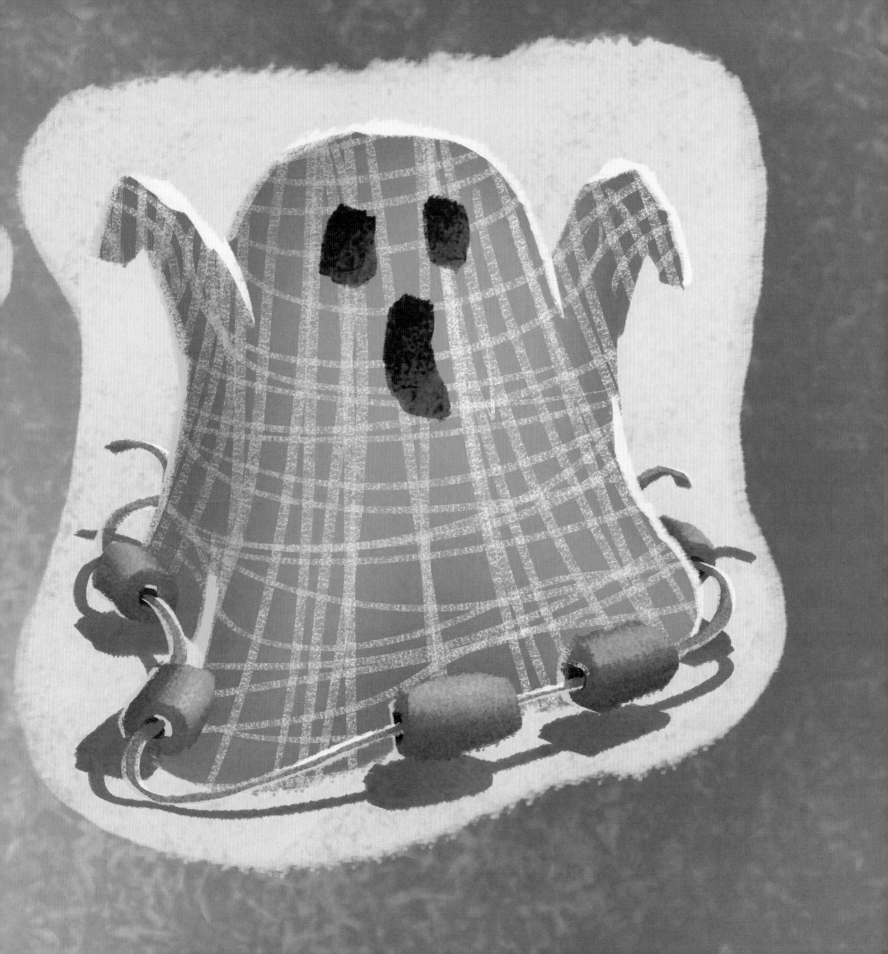

Suddenly, Dolly the Dolphin jumped
up next to the Eco Boat.

"HELP! Please! My friends Oli, Tom, and Will are trapped in ghost nets."

"Quick! Take us there now!"
shouted Sam.

They found Oli the Octopus, Tom the Turtle, and Will the Whale, terribly tangled in old fishing nets.

At once, Sam stretched out his robotic arms.

**CLICK...CLICK...CLICK...**

"Come on everyone, let's pull and shake the net hard together!"

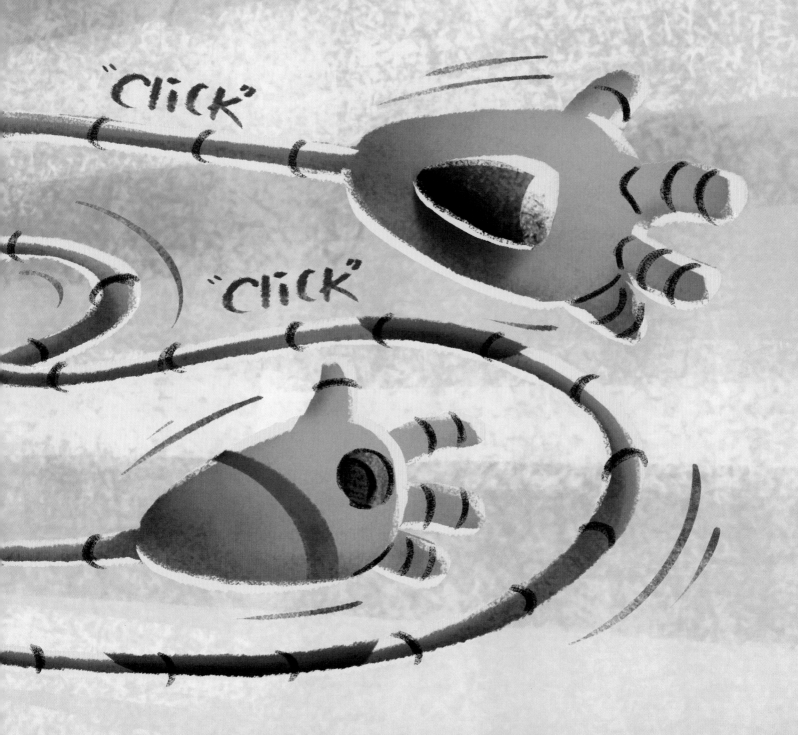

"ONE...TWO...THREE, PULL!" Sam shouted.

"ARRRRGGGGG!"

Again and again, they pulled and shook as hard as they could to free the animals.

But it was no good.

"It's just stuck," Sam shouted. "I can't get closer to them with the boat."

"And if the boat's propellers get tangled, we will all be in big trouble!" said Sam.

"Oh no! What are we going to do?" cried Jen.

"Please hurry, Sam! They don't look well!" shouted Dolly the Dolphin.

Sam thought and thought, then shouted out,

He twirled and twirled and stretched himself, spread out his arms, and transformed into a drone!

"Whoooaaa! Look at him go!" shouted Jack, grabbing the control of the boat.

Sam took off and flew over Oli and Will.

He transformed his hand into a clipper.

**"Hold on, Oli. Hold on, Will!"** shouted Sam.

**CUT! CUT! PLOP! PLOP!**

Oli and Will plopped free into the sea!

"Hurry! Young Tom is still stuck!" said Will the Whale.

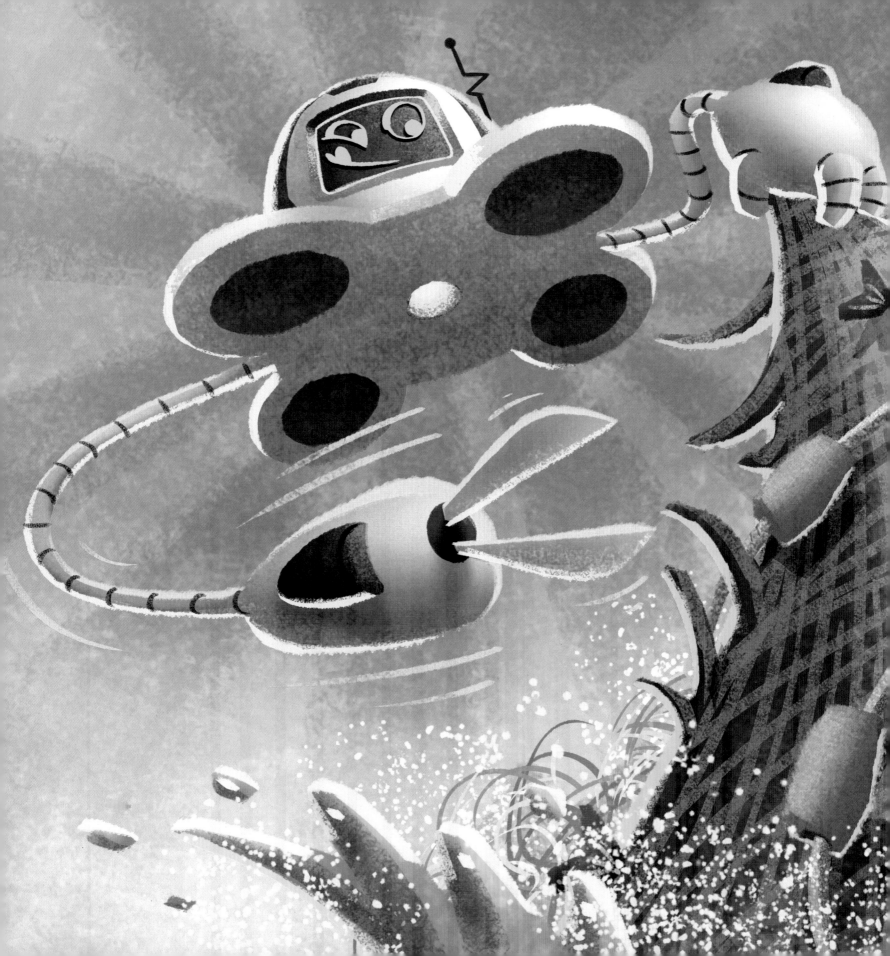

Tom was wiggling and jiggling in the ghost net.
Suddenly, Tom saw something soft and white floating by his mouth.
"Yummy, a jellyfish for me!"

But just as he opened his mouth, Dolly the Dolphin shouted, "Noooo, Tom! That's not a jellyfish. Don't eat it."

But it was too late!

"Gloob…Gloob…" Tom gobbled down half of a soft plastic shopping bag!

Right away, Tom cried,
"Uuuughhh, I don't feel very well."

Sam rushed to free Tom and grabbed his flipper, reached into his mouth, and pulled out the whole plastic bag!

"See? That's what you ate, Tom. That's what got you sick," Sam said.

**BUUURRRPP!!!**

Tom gave a loud burp, took a big gulp of air, and smiled happily.

Now Tom, Oli, and Will are safe and free.
"Thank you, Sam! Thank you, Dolly!" said the three.

They waved goodbye and swam away.

The children, the people, and the fisherman who were watching Sam from the beach clapped and cheered!

"Well, let's do one more thing," said Sam. "Let's get rid of the ghost nets that trapped Tom, Oli, and Will."

Thank you!

Sam pulled out a long hose and vacuumed the ghost nets and plastics into the belly of his Eco Boat.

Jen and Jack looked inside at the icky jumble through the glass window of the machine.

"Uggh," said Jen. "It's so creepy and messy."

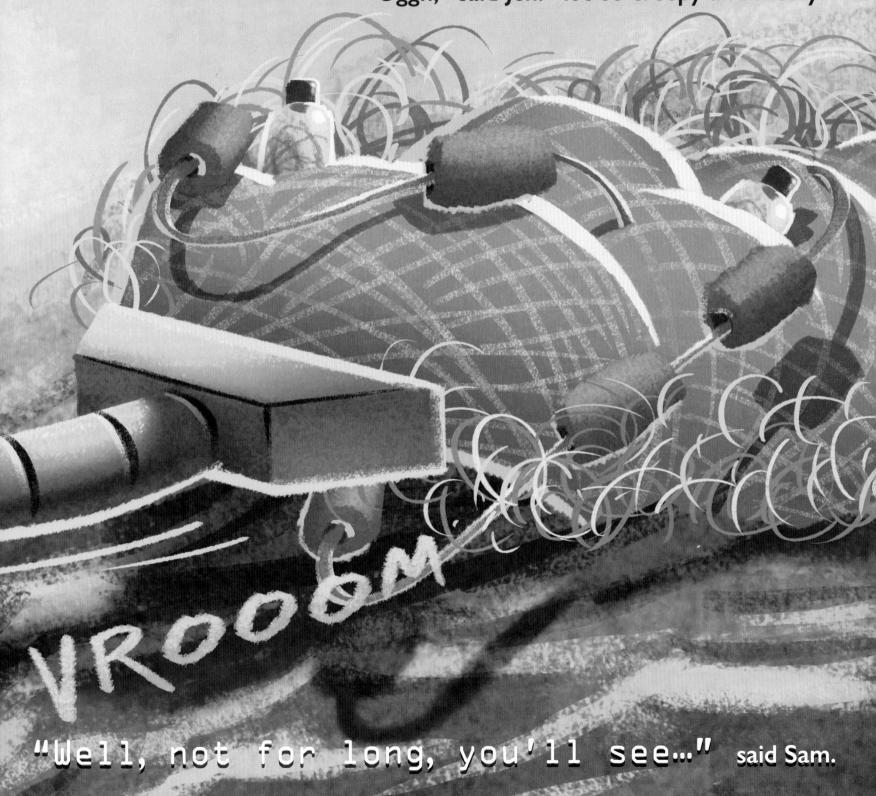

VROOOM

"Well, not for long, you'll see…" said Sam.

Sam stopped the Eco Boat at the pier and switched on the upcycling machines.

It whirred and purred, then chopped and whopped, and whirred over and over again.

Suddenly, it stopped…

And colorful plastic bins and toys poured out!

"Whoooaaa, so cool! The trash became toys!" Jack jumped up and down!

The children on the beach ran to Sam and shouted,
"Yay! You saved the animals."

"We want to be Eco Heroes like you!"

The children continued, "Can we help you pick up plastics on the beaches, so they won't harm the animals?"

"Yes, you can!" said Sam.

Sam gave them colorful bins to help.

The children raced up and down along the beach and picked up all the plastics.

Sam gave recycled toys and Eco Hero badges to the children.

"Sam!" called the fisherman.

"I saw what you did from the beach. Here are my old fishing nets and buoys.

Can you recycle them too? I don't want to hurt the animals," said the fisherman.

"Yes, of course!"

Sam put the old fishing nets and buoys in the machine.
Out came a new buoy this time!

"Here, take it. It's yours!"

"Really? For me? Thank you!" said the fisherman.

"We can turn plastics and old fishing nets into pellets and yarns to make many new things like toys, clothes, and more," explained Sam.

"I'll never throw my fishing gear in the sea again!"
said the fisherman as he waved goodbye.

The children gathered around Sam. "Please, we want more bins for our friends in the cities so they can be Eco Heroes too."

"What a great idea!" said Sam. "They will help stop plastics from getting into the rivers and the oceans in the first place."

Then everyone sang together: (to the tune of *"Old MacDonald Had a Farm"*)

"Eco Heroes saved the world,  E-I-E-I-O!
And on the beach, there were plastics,  E-I-E-I-O!

So we picked, picked here...
And we picked, picked there...

Here we picked, there we picked,
Everywhere we picked, picked.

Eco Heroes saved the world,  E-I-E-I-O
And now the seas are plastic-free,  E-I-E-I-O!"

# Scientific Information for Parents and Teachers

- Forty-six percent of the trash in the Great Pacific Garbage Patch is from ghost nets, crab pots, fish traps, buoys, and other fishing gears. *(Source: Dr. George Leonard, Ocean Conservancy's Chief Scientist)*

- Fifty-two percent of sea turtles worldwide have accidentally eaten plastics in the ocean. They thought plastic bags were jellyfish. *(Source: The US National Oceanic and Atmospheric Administration (NOAA))*

- Eight million tons of plastic trash enter the ocean every year. This is like dropping one garbage truck full of plastic trash into the ocean every minute or throwing two Empire State Buildings filled with plastics into the ocean every month. *(Source: National Geographic Kids)*

1. Where does all this plastic in the ocean come from?

   - People littering.

   - Improper disposal of trash in towns and cities.

   - Old, broken fishing gear left as trash or lost in the ocean by commercial fishing boats. This makes up over forty-six percent of the Great Pacific Garbage Patch.

2. How does domestic plastic get into rivers or oceans?

   - Rain and wind can sweep plastic items into nearby storm drains. From there, they flow into rivers, and from there, into oceans. Plastics can also block city storm drain systems and cause floods.

3. How do we become Eco Heroes and help save marine animals and reduce plastics in the oceans?

   - Never throw plastic items out from car windows or leave plastic trash at public areas, such as schools, parks, lakes, beaches, or at events such as music festivals, sports events, or any outdoor activities or gatherings. Dispose of them in proper bins or take them home. Invite others to do the same. This simple action alone can help save thousands of marine animals and birds, such as sea turtles, dolphins, whales, seals, sea birds, and more.

   - Choose reusable, refillable, or biodegradable containers to reduce the use of plastics.

   - Buy washing machines with special filters that can catch loose fibers and plastics. Our clothes shed tiny microfibers—synthetic yarns in our clothes—which go down the drain and end up in our waterways when we do laundry.

# ROBOTS FOR GOOD

Robots are often made to do jobs that are too hard, difficult, or dangerous for humans to do, such as firefighting or cleaning up oil spills and plastic trash in the oceans.

One example of a plastic cleaning robot is the Interceptor, created by a non-governmental organization (NGO) called Ocean Cleanup. The Interceptor is an unmanned surface vehicle (USV) that collects plastics at the mouth of rivers before they get into the ocean.

The Ocean Cleanup team also collects trash from the Great Pacific Garbage Patch using a system called "Wilson." Their goal is to try to clean an area equivalent to 500,000 soccer fields.

The team collects and recycles ocean plastics and ghost nets and turns them into cool sunglasses.

# ACKNOWLEDGMENTS

I would like to thank:

Mr. Anthony Ziccardi, my publisher, for having found Sam and immediately passing it on to the kind and super-efficient Megan Wheeler. It was a pleasure to work with this amazing team, especially Kate Monahan, my very patient manager, and Devon Brown, for everything she does that makes this book a great success.

I would like to thank Tom (5), Oli (8), William (11) and their mum, Anna Ruggles-Brise, my Beta readers. Their enthusiastic feedback provided me with much encouragement.

Finally, I'd like to thank everyone no matter their age, who strives to find ways, big or small, to make a change, to salvage our blue planet, stop the path toward destruction that we are on, and build a sustainable future for all.

I believe man-made problems can be solved by us, when we are willing to do so.


Thassanee W. Wanick

# FUN FACTS ABOUT THE AUTHOR

- Thassanee ice trekked the Glacier of the Andes in Patagonia, at the southern tip of South America.

- She rode a buffalo and an elephant in Thailand, a Himalayan Cashmere goat cart in India, a camel in Egypt, horses in Brazil, and drove a dog sled 500 km above the Arctic Circle in Norway.

- Thassanee adopted a baby elephant, Nong Lychee and her mom who were wandering in the city of Bangkok eating from trash cans. They now live in the lush forest in northern Thailand, under the care of the Golden Triangle Asian Elephant Foundation led by Mr. John E. Roberts.

- She is a qualified boat skipper and a PADI-certified diver.

- As a biologist, she studied coral reefs and turtles in Mexico and mangroves in Thailand.

- She has traveled to fifty countries and has lived in eight countries.

# ABOUT THE AUTHOR

*Photo by Thomas Susemihl*

A diplomat with a passion for the environment, Hon. Consul General Thassanee W. Wanick holds a master's degree in Environmental Studies from the University of Pennsylvania.

She became a well-known expert in business and sustainability and was a professor of sustainable economics for the MBA program at the Tec de Monterrey, Mexico during her sabbatical. She was also a guest lecturer at the Wharton School of the University of Pennsylvania.

She is the founder and first chair of the board of the Green Building Council Brazil and a former board member of the World Green Building Council.

She has been a lecturer and speaker in various government and business events including the first Wharton-UN Global Compact International Conference, UN Habitat, International Biofuels Conference, the Petroleum Authority of Thailand, CEMEX University Television Broadcast, the World Bank-IFC's Sustainable Finance launch of the Sustainability Index of the Brazilian Stock Exchange, and the 2nd International Forum on Sustainability in the Amazon. Among the other speakers were former President Bill Clinton, Governor Arnold Schwarzenegger, Sir Richard Branson, and Mr. James Cameron, filmmaker.

She created and organized a campaign to fight global warming called One Degree Less in partnership with Dr. Akbari from the Lawrence Berkeley National Laboratory, California Energy Commissioner Dr. Arthur Rosenfeld, CNN international, ROLEX Sailing Week, and more to help reduce the temperature of the planet, using white reflective cool roofs and surfaces.

Celsius, the giant polar bear mascot of the campaign, became a beloved character for adults and schoolchildren alike.

She was a keynote speaker during the First Green Inaugural Ball of President Barack Obama in 2009, Washington, D.C.

Thassanee was awarded the Royal Honour of "Commander of the Most Noble Order of the Crown," bestowed by His Majesty the King of Thailand.

She attended a private presentation and dinner hosted by His Royal Highness The Prince of Wales to discuss sustainable urban development at St. James Palace, London, England.